VICTORY ★ SCHOOL SUPERSTARS

STONE ARCH BOOKS
a capstone imprint

Sports
Illustrated KIDS

Beach Volleyball
Is No Joke

by Anita Yasuda
illustrated by Jorge Santillan

STONE ARCH BOOKS
a capstone imprint

VICTORY
SCHOOL
SUPERSTARS

Sports Illustrated KIDS *Beach Volleyball Is No Joke*
is published by Stone Arch Books — A Capstone Imprint
151 Good Counsel Drive, P.O. Box 669
Mankato, Minnesota 56002
www.capstonepub.com

Art Director: Bob Lentz
Graphic Designer: Hilary Wacholz
Production Specialist: Michelle Biedscheid

Timeline photo credits: Shutterstock/Katherine Welles
(middle right), Vahe Katrjyan (middle left); Sports Illustrated/
Bob Rosato (bottom right), John Biever (bottom left);
Wikipedia (top).

Printed in the United States of America in Stevens Point, Wisconsin.
032011   006111WZF11

Library of Congress Cataloging-in-Publication Data
Yasuda, Anita.
Beach volleyball is no joke / by Anita Yasuda ; illustrated by Jorge H.
Santillan.
  p. cm. — (Sports Illustrated kids. Victory School superstars)
Summary: Instead of trying to learn beach volleyball, Tyler spends a week at
camp pulling practical jokes, only to upset his teammates.
ISBN 978-1-4342-2232-9 (library binding)
ISBN 978-1-4342-3393-6 (pbk.)
  1. Beach volleyball—Juvenile fiction. 2. Volleyball—Juvenile fiction.
3. Practical jokes—Juvenile fiction. 4. Teamwork (Sports)—Juvenile fiction.
[1. Beach volleyball—Fiction. 2. Volleyball—Fiction. 3. Practical jokes—
Fiction. 4. Teamwork (Sports)—Fiction.] I. Santillan, Jorge, ill. II. Title. III.
Series: Sports Illustrated kids. Victory School superstars.
PZ7.Y2124Be 2011
[Fic]—dc22   2011002310

TABLE of CONTENTS

TYLER TROFEE

Beach Volleyball

AGE: 10
GRADE: 4
SUPER SPORTS ABILITY: Super Shooting

Playa Victoria Superstars:

JOSH CARMEN TYLER

PLAYA VICTORIA

Don't let Playa Victoria's relaxed vibe fool you. Here, athletes work hard as they soak up the rays. The best of the best train at this gorgeous beach resort. Learn summer sports like beach volleyball, wakeboarding, and surfing from the top experts.

1. Surf Shack
2. Volleyball Court
3. Main Boat Dock
4. Resort Lodge
5. Bungalows

Morning Surprise

The screen door creaks open as I slip
out of the cabin. *This is going to be great*, I
think. My plan is going well until — *CRASH*
— I bump into a pile of surfboards. In a
snap, the snoring stops and the yelling
begins.

"Tylerrrrrrrrr!" they all yell at the same
time.

I guess my roommates found their morning surprise — a handful of shaving cream for each of them.

"Just wait until I get my hands on him!" one of them shouts.

I jump over the porch railing and dash across the beach. Playa Victoria, a resort for kids gifted in sports, is a blast! This is the best school trip ever.

I am lucky to be a student at the Victory School for Super Athletes. My skill is in basketball. No matter how I shoot the ball, it sails through the hoop. With my skill, tossing shoes up on the roof is a piece of cake. Just like in basketball, I can't miss.

The resort's motto is "Where friendship begins, and sports never end." When I leave, that last part will change to "and jokes never end."

"There he is," yells Kevin from my basketball team. "Get him!"

I dodge the guys with a fake out — left, right, left. I love goofing off like this. I wish I could play pranks all day. But I am here to learn some new sports, starting with beach volleyball.

"Fancy handling skills aren't going to help you now," says Kevin, trying to grab his shoe.

"We'll see about that," I reply.

I don't give it back to the basketball team's all-star passer. Instead, I blow right past him. With a snap of my wrist, the shoe goes up, up, and away. All Kevin can do is watch.

"I'm going to get you good," he warns.

"You'll need your shoes to catch me," I say, running away with a laugh.

CHAPTER 2

Less Fooling Around

Cyclists and skaters jam the boardwalk.
I weave in and out. I can't miss skills class
again.

Stephanie, the volleyball pro, waves
me over. She's the resort's beach volleyball
expert, and she's here to teach us the basics
of the game.

"Tyler, do you know how I learned to play beach volleyball?" she asks, folding her arms.

I think back to what I did last night. "By shining a flashlight into the girls' cabin and yelling 'truck?'" I ask with a big grin.

"Yeah," growls my teammate Alicia, who is on the cheerleading squad. "You're a joke a minute."

Stephanie sighs and shakes her head.

"Practice," she says. "Tyler, I need to see more volleyball and less fooling around."

She points to a pile of balls. All the air has been let out. They look like this morning's pancakes. I give her my "not me" look.

"How are we going to play now?" asks Alicia.

"This isn't school, Alicia," I say. "It's just camp."

"No," she says, "It's a *sports* camp. We are here to learn new skills."

I don't bother getting into it with her. I just get busy pumping up the balls.

Practice Time

The next morning, Stephanie runs us through countless drills. Shuffling back and forth across the sand, I pass to Alicia. We don't pause for a second. To make it harder, Stephanie has us pass lower.

"You can do this!" she yells.

Next we play a game called "pass the pepper." We have to pass, set, dig, and hit to each other. Alicia starts the drill with a nice easy toss. I get into position. My arms are stretched out.

"Nice, Tyler," Stephanie says. "Try bending your knees more."

"No problem," I say.

Smack! My volleyball zings Stephanie in the side.

Sorry, I mouth. I don't know what's wrong. I am usually pretty good at any sport.

"Keep playing," Stephanie says. "Tyler, position two this time."

"Okay," I reply, even though I'm not sure what she means.

When did we learn about position two? Was it the day I plastic wrapped the girls' toilets? Or the day the cooks' aprons went up the flagpole?

After I miss the ball for a third time, Stephanie calls me over. "Watch the others for a bit," she says.

"Fine," I say. I plop down on the hot sand. Then I start thinking about what I would rather be doing. Swimming would be nice. Hiding the mess hall chairs would be better.

Honk! An air horn blows. I am so happy to hear that sound.

"Lunchtime!" I shout. "Last one to the mess hall eats mystery meat."

"Shouldn't we practice more?" Alicia calls after me.

"What for? It's easy," I yell over my shoulder.

Blanket Volleyball

At lunch, Stephanie comes over to our table. She hands us some photos. "This afternoon's activity is a mystery," she says. "See you at the beach."

Alicia and I go over the clues. The photos are of a blanket and a beach ball. "Awesome," I say. "We have the afternoon off."

"Dream on, Tyler," says Alicia. "You might want to try harder. Our first game is in four days."

I shrug. I'm not worried about the game. I'm good at sports. I don't have to work hard at basketball. In fact, I can lazily toss the ball toward the hoop, and it always goes in.

At the beach, Stephanie splits us into teams for blanket volleyball. We have to use a blanket to throw and catch the ball.

"Like beach volleyball," Stephanie says, "this game needs teamwork, too."

Alicia, Kevin, and I are on one team. The other team wins the coin toss, so we get ready by the net. The ball keeps falling off their blanket. At last, they launch it into the air. We run for it and miss. Then we miss again.

"Work as a team!" Stephanie shouts.

I have a better idea. If this was basketball, fans would distract the shooter. Chants and goofy faces are the way to go. This will be fun!

The ball is lying on the blanket. I cross my eyes while I chant, "Bump, set, hit, spike. Put it in my hand."

"Up in space. In your face," I shout as we use the blanket to toss the ball into the air. "Drop it in the . . ."

"SAND!" I shout. I pull sharply to the left. Alicia and Kevin go right. *Thunk!* We all end up on the ground.

I let out a big laugh before I notice how mad my team is. Alicia is glaring at me. Kevin won't meet my eyes. Stephanie simply sighs.

"Come on," I say. "There are worse things than sand sandwiches."

Alicia shoves past me. "Everything is a joke to you," she mumbles. "But to me, beach volleyball is no joke."

CHAPTER 5

Time to Learn

The group takes off for the showers. No one gives me eye contact.

"Tyler," calls Stephanie. "Can I talk to you?"

"They're pretty mad at me," I say.

Stephanie nods. "Jokes are okay at times," she says. "But your friends came here to learn a new sport. Didn't you?"

"Sure," I say looking down at my feet.

She has a point. Maybe I should spend less time playing jokes, and more time learning beach volleyball. "Sorry for being a goof," I say.

"It's okay," she says smiling. "I know you will work hard from here on out."

"I will," I promise. "Would you be able to help me get up to speed?"

Stephanie agrees to practice with me. We pass and volley back and forth by the nets. Slowly, I get the hang of it.

"Now can I try serving?" I ask.

"You bet," Stephanie says. "It's one of the most important parts of the game."

Throwing the ball above my head, I try to hit it. This is an overhand serve. It seems simple but it isn't. I try again and again.

"Hey, Tyler, I think a kid like you needs a little fun to go with his work," says Stephanie.

"What do you mean?" I ask.

"Try serving this," says Stephanie, throwing me one of the big beach balls from earlier.

I throw the ball as high as I can. *Thwack!* It's a good strong hit and finally a serve makes it over the net. "That was awesome!" I say. "It's so light, that I can really slam it."

After a few more minutes of serving the beach ball, I trade it in for the volleyball. My serve sails over the net.

"Way to go, Tyler!" I hear someone say.

It's Alicia. She and Kevin have been watching the whole time. I sure am happy to see them. "Do you think we can practice together?" I ask cautiously.

Kevin runs over. "Sure, but . . ."

"No more jokes," Alicia adds sternly.

"Okay," I say. "And thanks."

For the last drill, they join in. We lie down on the sand in a pile. Stephanie blows her whistle. She tosses the ball high. Scrambling up, we take turns passing, setting, and hitting.

"Good teamwork," Stephanie yells.

When practice breaks up I feel great. Alicia gives me a push into the sand. "Last one to the mess hall eats mystery meat," she calls.

The Big Match

I am ready for today's match. Over the week, Alicia, Kevin, and I practiced on the beach until dark. It's been fun.

I even trained before breakfast against a wall. I tossed the ball with my left hand and hit it with my right. It was perfect until the cooks told me to cut it out before all the eggs got scrambled.

Now, it is time to put my new skills to use. I spot Stephanie walking toward me. She is smiling as she greets me.

"Well," says Stephanie trying not to laugh, "I told you to come prepared, but I don't think you need the facial hair."

Puzzled, I look at my reflection in one of the tide pools. Stretching from ear to ear is a curly moustache made with a black marker. My guess is that Kevin is the artist!

"Kevin got me back good," I say, smiling. Then I look up and spot my teammates. Both Kevin and Alicia have moustaches, too!

"We're a team, remember," Alicia says.

Kevin nods, giving his moustache a pretend twirl.

Before the match begins, we tie on our Victory bandanas. My heart pumps loudly. *Just breathe*, I tell myself.

The game is about to begin. The other team rushes onto the court. They are huge. Plus they have special abilities just like us. They are going to jump higher, hit harder, and move quicker than regular kids.

"Let's do this," I say.

I run. I jump. I dive. The game is incredibly fast. Both teams win a set.

In the third set, Alicia is a real threat. She jumps so high, her feet are above the net. She touches the ball at the same time as another player. But Alicia manages to tip it over.

Now it is coming right back at us. Kevin sets the ball for me.

"It's mine!" I shout.

I picture the beach ball from yesterday, and I leap for it. This team is about to learn how dangerous my smash can be. My raised hand makes contact.

The ball flies over the net slamming into the ground. *Yes!* Sand flies into the air. And for once I am not eating it. The match is ours!

"You did it!" Alicia shouts.

"No, *we* did it," I reply.

"Way to go!" Stephanie cheers.

As we walk back to the resort, I feel tomorrow is going to be even better. "Hey, guys, maybe the Playa Victoria ghost will be at the fire ring tonight," I say.

"Ghost?" Alicia asks puzzled.

"He means ghosts," Kevin says smiling.

"And I know just where we can get some sheets," I say.

"Stephanie's bunk!" we yell.

49

GLOSSARY

bandanas (ban-DAN-uhz)—large, brightly colored handkerchiefs

bunk (BUHNGK)—a narrow bed

cyclists (SYE-kuhl-ists)—people who ride bicycles

incredibly (in-KRED-uh-blee)—very or extremely

lazily (LAY-zuh-lee)—without work or effort

mumbles (MUHM-buhls)—speaks quietly and unclearly

resort (ri-ZORT)—a place where people go for rest and relaxation

scrambling (SKRAM-buh-ling)—rushing or struggling to get somewhere

shrug (SHRUHG)—to raise your shoulders in order to show doubt or lack of interest

shuffling (SHUHF-uh-ling)—moving while hardly raising your feet from the floor or ground

sternly (STERN-lee)—strictly or harshly

usually (YOO-zhoo-uh-lee)—normally

ABOUT THE AUTHOR

ANITA YASUDA

Anita Yasuda is the published author of several children's books. She and her family live in Southern Ontario. When she is not writing, she is hiking with her dog Ted, playing tetherball, or planning a new adventure. Anita is also the author of *There's No Crying in Baseball* from the Victory School Superstars.

ABOUT THE ILLUSTRATOR

JORGE SANTILLAN

Jorge Santillan got his start illustrating in the children's sections of local newspapers. He opened his own illustration studio in 2005. His creative team specializes in books, comics, and children's magazines. Jorge lives in Mendoza, Argentina, with his wife, Bety; son, Luca; and their four dogs, Fito, Caro, Angie, and Sammy.

BEACH VOLLEYBALL IN HISTORY

1895 William G. Morgan creates the game of volleyball in Holyoke, Massachusetts.

1915 **Men's teams** reportedly play volleyball on the beach in Hawaii.

1920s Volleyball courts are set up on the beach in Santa Monica, California. Players play six on a team.

1930s The first two-man beach volleyball game is played in Santa Monica.

1965 The California Beach Volleyball Association is formed.

1987 The first Beach Volleyball World Championship is played in **Brazil**.

1996 Beach volleyball becomes an Olympic sport at the **Atlanta games**.

2007 American **Misty May-Treanor** becomes the women's all-time wins leader in beach volleyball.

2008 **Misty May-Treanor** and **Kerri Walsh** win gold at the Beijing Olympics, becoming the first team ever to repeat as gold medalists.

Tyler Trofee Takes Home the Gold!

If you liked Tyler's beach volleyball adventure, check out his other sports stories.

Nobody Wants to Play with a Ball Hog

In basketball, Tyler is a perfect shot. Since he can't miss, he quits passing to his teammates. The other boys are sick of how Tyler plays. When will he learn that nobody wants to play with a ball hog?

There's No Crying in Baseball

The Victory School students have challenged their teachers to a game of baseball. No one is more excited than Tyler. But when he sprains his ankle, he doesn't even want to go to the game. Maybe he forgot that there's no crying in baseball.

STONE ARCH BOOKS
a capstone imprint